Laurel *for* Libby

First published in 2006 by the Bodleian Library
Broad Street, Oxford, OX1 3BG

www. bodleianbookshop.co.uk

ISBN 1 85124 350 X
ISBN 13 978 85124 350 1

Cover design by Dot Little
Printed and bound by L.E.G.O. S.p.A., Vicenza, Italy
A CIP record of this publication is available from the British
Library

Reproduced from Bodleian Library, MS. Eng. d. 3627

Foreword

Graham Greene was an undergraduate at Balliol
College, Oxford, when he met and fell in love with
the beautiful Vivienne Dayrell-Browning, a nine-
teen-year-old poet who worked for the bookseller
Basil Blackwell. They married on 15 October 1927
and during the course of the next ten years Greene
began writing the novels which made him famous,
while Vivien (as she preferred to be known) pursued
her interests in Victoriana and her world-renowned
collection of dolls' houses.

On the night of 14 September 1937 Vivien had
a dream about a mysteriously long-lived 'deeply
purred and furred' tabby cat and when she woke up
the next day she wrote *Laurel for Libby,* the story of
'The Oldest Cat in Bristol'. Libby's tale spans nearly
three-quarters of a century, from 1862 until the eve
of the Second World War, and involves its *Orlando*-
like protagonist in several changes of name and
periodically fluctuating gender, although whether
known as Libby, Methuselah, Kitty, Don, Tom, Moë
or Queenie 'all the time it was the same cat, that's
the important thing'.

Vivien and Graham on their wedding day

Vivien then spent several days copying the manuscript into a notebook that she had specially bound and covered in silver, pink and white metallic-effect paper, illustrating it throughout with woodcuts ingeniously executed in several media, the most effective of which – according to her meticulous bibliographical notes – turned out to be Bronco toilet paper. Finally, after a month's work and just in time for their wedding anniversary, she presented *Laurel for Libby* to Graham, the 'onlie begetter of Lucy Caroline and Francis Charles [their children] THIS that I made by myself … On our tenth Anniversary 1927 – October 15 – 1937'.

The vividly coloured manuscript notebook remained in Vivien's possession at the time of her death, when it was given to the Bodleian Library by the antiquarian booksellers, Waterfield's, on the occasion of what would have been her 100th birthday in 2004.

The text in this facsimile edition has been reproduced at 83% of the original size.

Judith Priestman

13 All Saints Road, Clifton

LAUREL ~ FOR ~ LIBBY ~

She was born in the year of the second Great Exhibition and she was run over by a trades-man's bicycle in 1934 — a long life for a cat. There were all sorts of mysteries about her.. whether she was male or female, for instance. and where she went when she ran away in '69: she came back perfectly happy and sleek with a new ribbon round her neck: but all the time it was the same cat, that's the important thing, and that is what can be proved by unbroken human tradition, which when all is said and done, is usually the final proof of anything. Think of the Battle of Hastings.

Her placid history was so well-known that it was positively certain that she had never had any kittens (unless she had them when she ran away) Possibly this has some connection with her longevity: she may have been the only recorded female cat that did not have kittens. If she was a female. Not having kittens made it more difficult to be certain.

The curious thing is that it wasn't until about the end of the last century that anyone thought it worth while to comment on her. She'd been about, of course, recognizably the same, ever since the family could remember, but my grandmother, who was an antiquarian and very interested in gothic, was the first to notice what a remarkable person Libby was. At this period of her life the cat was called Libby: it was confusing that a succession of cooks named her (or him, as some considered) as she was handed on like an heirloom. When a cook didn't re-name her and the old name lapsed, she was usually called after the last cook, as in this case. My grandmother showed the then Libby at a Ladies Sale of Work, held at the Victoria Rooms, Clifton: the social histor--ian could date it fairly accurately

because the stall where she sat
sold pleated satin table centres
and small plush monkeys for
decorating mantlepieces. A
hand-painted card nearby held
the words "THE OLDEST CAT IN
BRISTOL", a modest claim, one
realised on reading further ~
"Born in the summer of 1862, and
has lived in the same family all
her life."

This record, as it would now
be called, was all the more
remarkable because, except for
my grandmother and myself who
was priviledged to know Methusalah (as she was then known)
in old age, the Armytage family
really did not like cats. The males
must have owned at least twenty
dogs during the cat's lifetime.

Arlington Crescent.

She stayed in this house for the enormous period of thirty-one years, from 1881 to 1912. Here she was called Libby, then for a short time Don (and sometimes Tom) by a cook who believed her to be male: then a new cook came who asked the parlourmaid what the cat was called and was told "Libby, after Mrs Libby." This was the time when the cat was exhibited at the Christmas Sale of Work. Soon after, Libby caught some throat infection which resulted in a very hoarse cry, and in joke she was called Moë, which was what it sounded like ~ a reminiscence of the milkman's cry in the quiet squares of Clifton.

About the turn of the century Moë
grew a little stiff in the legs and
rather stout, and when the queen
died it seemed appropriate to the
Kitchen staff to rename her "Queenie"
~"It's not as if Moë was her right
name", ~ and so she remained
until my grandfather, who disliked
Womens' Suffrage and didn't care
for cats, said, the day that she
was sick on the rockingchair
"Mrs Pankhurst's her name."

This was too recondite for the
cook and Queenie was her name
where she got her meals.

Queenie took part in several
"Guess her Weight" competitions in

Red Cross Bazaars and began to have a local fame. My uncle Peter on leave said, "Hullo: Methusalah still with us?" and surprisingly, by unspoken consent the whole family called the cat Methusalah from that day on, and after he was killed it was clear that she would never change her name again.

In 1912 my grandparents had moved into a rather small brown brick Georgian house on the wrong side of Clifton. Their family had left home many years before and it was their second and last move: 13 All Saints' Road was sold; the cook and two housemaids came with them and so did Queenie and a large cage of canaries and Tim.

.. Early croquet ...

Kitty's early life. The other photo-
graph was taken during the
War and showed the grand-
parents, the dog of the moment,
and Methusalah standing in
the porch with the five-hundred-
weight crate of (I think) plum-
stones which had been collected
for the National Salvage
Council.

I come reluctantly to describe
the creature herself. She was
always 'Cat' or 'Queenie' to me,
and female. Methusalah and
masculinity contradicted every
implication of her moon-like pale
green eyes, her rotund form:
she gave me the impression of
a very heavy square fur

cushion, or an object almost of the weight and consistency of treacle — something, in short, that had to be scooped up at the edges if I make myself clear.

She was deeply furred and purred: a richly-marked tabby with a silvery muzzle: this, with her rather touching weakness of sometimes dribbling a little, was the only external sign of her age. But once I prized open those gentle jaws and gazed down them reverently: her mouth was pink and empty as a new-born kittens'. She had never had any marked idiocyncracies: one could not work her up as a "character": my grandmother said she always came in to morning prayers and sat by the cook: otherwise she did not mingle much with the family ~ until I came, I am proud and happy to think. At Christmas and at Easter and sometimes at half-term I came, and usually in time for late tea, and the cat decended from the hot-water tank upstairs and sat on my serge knees: bliss and content for me anyway.

In 1922 my grandmother died: for some reason my youngest aunt decided to be responsible for Methusalah and took her to London.

Bibliographical Note.

This story was based on a dream
of Sept. 14 and all the names
except the National Salvage Council
and Arlington Crescent were put
in when I wrote it next day.
I checked some details later: a
letter from M·R·G· Sept. 17, says
"I can find nothing about old
croquet in the Ency. Brit: it came
to England in 1856 or possibly
earlier. I remember that two hoops
were crossed over each other in
the middle and the bell hung there,
but whether one had to make it
ring or not I don't remember ...
·· Pelargoniums were very popular...
·· Fuchias of course, and begonias.
That pretty blue plumbago grew all

over the conservatory in an aunt's house, inside. Pink geraniums of course. Maidenhair fern was thought essential to any bunch of flowers.

In the '80s would be safe for the plush monkeys: in the '80s and perhaps early '90s articles worked in crewel stitch were popular at bazaars. We worked as children antimaccassars with designs taken from Miss Kate Greenaways books ... painted drainpipes for umbrellas were in the '80s or even '70s I should think .."

~

The paper for the binding was bought at Kettles' and the book, a plain exercise book was cut to size by Mr Smart, who also bound it. Great disappointment was caused when he wrote: "You ask for 32 pp. I expect you *mean* 32 LEAVES ~ 64 pages: many people make this mistake." It was not a mistake, and consequently a number of pages had to be torn out, so spoiling the appearance of the book. Sepia water colour paint was chosen for printing (not tried before.) It was most unsatisfactory but shortness of time precluded reprinting. A great number of proofs were pulled on Heintze & Blankerts (Berlin) printing paper with no success and it was decided to use Bronco. Lino is a very cheeselike substance in comparison with wood ~ it has no resistance and the white lines

must be cut very coarsely in
order to prevent them from
inking.   A great many had to
be recut, after seeing proof pulls,
which made the illustrations
worse than ever.

In any case of course there is
no ratio between the time —
some sixty hours ~ and trouble
taken, and the result.
But it is offered with much
affection.

Sept 15 - October 14.
        1937.
Tenth wedding anneversary, October 15: 1937.

38

Presented to
Graham Greene
by his wife
Vivien Greene .